This book belongs to

....

....

FREDERICK WARNE
Published by the Penguin Group
Penguin Books Ltd, 80 Strand, London WC2R 0RL, England
Penguin Books Australia Ltd,
250 Camberwell Road, Camberwell, Victoria 3124, Australia
New York, Canada, India, New Zealand, South Africa
First published by Frederick Warne 2006
Previously published by Ladybird Books 2004, 2005
18 17 16 15 14 13 12 11
Copyright © Eric Hill, 2006
Eric Hill has asserted his moral rights under
the Copyright, Designs and Patents Act of 1988
All rights reserved
ISBN-13: 978-07232-5841-4
Planned and produced by Ventura Publishing Ltd
80 Strand, London WC2R 0RL
Printed in China

Spot's
Storytime
Collection

Eric Hill

Contents

Spot's
Garden

One sunny day, Spot was helping
Grandpa in the garden.
"This is so much fun, Grandpa,"
Spot said. "I think I'd like to have my
own bit of garden to grow things."

"That's a good idea, Spot," said Grandpa. "You can have the patch by the fence. It's nice and sunny." "Thank you, Grandpa!" said Spot.

"You'll need something to plant in your garden," said Grandpa. So he and Spot went to the shop to buy seeds.

"There are so many colourful seed packets," said Spot. "I can't decide which to choose."
"Carrots and lettuce are good to grow," said Grandpa. "And they taste delicious in salads."

Grandpa showed Spot how to dig
out rows for planting.
"The lettuces can go on one side,
and the carrots on the other,"
said Grandpa.

Spot made his rows nice and straight.

Then it was time to plant the seeds. Grandpa showed Spot how to sow the seeds in the rows they had dug.

"Tweet! Tweet!" called some birds,
as they flew down from the tree.
"I think the birds want to help us,
Grandpa," said Spot.

"I think the birds want to help
themselves – to the seeds!" laughed
Grandpa. "We'd better make a scarecrow
to keep them away."
With some wood from the shed,
and an old shirt, Grandpa and Spot
made a scarecrow.
"The scarecrow can have my hat,"
said Spot.

21

The next day, Spot went to water
his vegetable garden.

"Grandpa," he said, "I don't think
the scarecrow is working!"
"Oh dear!" said Grandpa.

23

"Why don't we give the birds some seeds of their own?" said Spot. "Then they won't need to eat mine." "That's a very good idea, Spot," said Grandpa. "I've got some sunflower seeds in the shed. Birds love sunflower seeds!"

25

Spot helped Grandpa fill a tray with
sunflower seeds and put them out
on a little table.
The birds seemed to like them much
more than Spot's vegetable seeds!

"Let's give the birds some water, too," said Spot, "in case all those sunflower seeds make them thirsty."

27

Spot watered his vegetable garden
every day. He carefully pulled out
the weeds, too.

Sometimes Steve and Helen came
to help. Soon Spot's vegetables
began to grow!

The plants in Spot's garden grew and
grew. At last the lettuces were ready
for picking.
"But where are the carrots?" Spot
asked Grandpa.

"Right here," said Grandpa,
"waiting for you." He showed Spot
how to loosen the soil and tug at
the carrot tops.
Up came the carrots!

"Look!" said Spot. "There's something else in my garden. How did they get here?"

"The birds must have dropped some of the seeds we gave them," said Grandpa, "and they grew into these lovely sunflowers."

Spot invited Steve and Helen to
come for a picnic lunch. Grandpa
made a salad with the lettuce from
the garden.
"Thank you all for helping me
with my garden," said Spot.

"And thank you for sharing your vegetables," said Steve and Helen.
"Tweet! Tweet!" said the birds.
"I think they're saying thank you, too!" laughed Grandpa.

Spot's
Show and Tell

Spot and his friends arrived at school bright and early.

"Good morning, everyone,"
said Miss Bear.
"Good morning,
Miss Bear,"
everyone replied.

When everyone was settled,
Miss Bear asked, "Does anyone
have anything special for
Show and Tell today?"

Helen and Tom both put their
hands up.

Miss Bear asked Helen to come
up first.

Helen held up her pink ballet shoes
for everyone to see. They had lovely
ribbons to keep them on her feet.

"Every week I go to ballet class,"
said Helen. "Next week we're
doing a concert and I'm going to
be a flower!"

Everyone thought Helen's ballet
shoes were very special. They all
clapped. Helen was very happy.

Next it was Tom's turn.
"I've brought my new kite," said
Tom. "It's very special. My dad
helped me to make it. We used
special paper, wooden sticks and
glue. We're going to fly it
on Saturday."

Everyone thought Tom's kite was
wonderful and they all clapped.
Tom was very happy.

Later that morning, it was time for painting. Spot and Steve shared an easel.

"I'm going to bring something for Show and Tell tomorrow," said Spot.

"Me too," said Steve. "But I'm not
sure what to bring."
"Neither am I," said Spot. "We'll
have to think hard, won't we?"

49

That afternoon, Steve was going to Spot's house to play. Sally picked Spot and Steve up and they all walked home together.

Steve saw a bright orange autumn leaf on the grass and he picked it up. "Maybe I'll take this for Show and Tell tomorrow," he said. "It's a lovely colour!"

When they got back, Spot and Steve
played cars in Spot's room.

"My car collection is special," Spot said to Steve. "Maybe I'll take my cars to Show and Tell tomorrow." "That's a good idea," said Steve.

At bedtime, Spot was still thinking about Show and Tell.

Suddenly, he had a great idea. "I know what I want to take to Show and Tell tomorrow," said Spot. "It's very, very special."
Spot whispered something to Sally.

"That sounds perfect!" said Sally, and
she kissed Spot goodnight.
"Sweet dreams, Spot!"

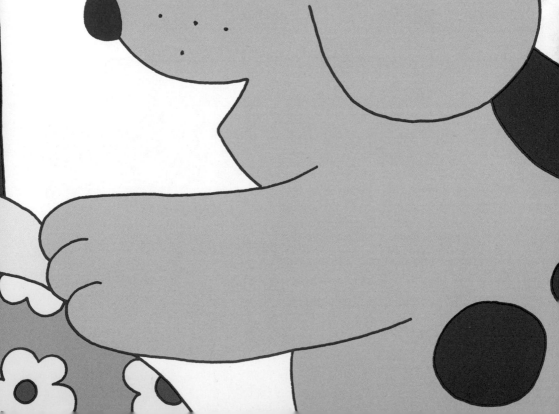

The next morning, Spot was smiling
and cheerful when he met Steve on
the way to school.
"Have you got something for Show
and Tell?" asked Steve.
"Yes," said Spot. "And it's very, very
special. Have you got something?"
"Yes," said Steve, happily.
"And it's very special, too."

At school, Miss Bear asked if anyone
had brought something special for
Show and Tell.

Spot and Steve put their hands up
and Miss Bear asked them to
come to the front of the class.

59

"I'd like to show the picture
I painted of my friend Spot!"
said Steve.
Spot laughed.
"And I'd like to show the picture
I painted of my friend Steve,"
said Spot.

Everyone clapped, even Miss Bear!
Spot and Steve were very, very happy!
"Both of our pictures are very special,"
said Spot, proudly.

Spot's
Camping Trip

One rainy morning, Spot looked
out of the window in Sally's room.
"Can I go out to play, Mum?"
he asked.

"I think it's too wet to play outdoors today," said Mum. "Then can Steve and Helen come here to play?" Spot asked. "Of course," said Mum. "Let's call them now."

A few minutes later, Steve and Helen were at the door. Both of them were very wet.

Spot helped his friends hang up
their raincoats and put away their
dripping umbrellas and wellies.

Spot and his friends went to Spot's room. They took all the toys out of the toy chest. They took all the games down from the shelf. But nobody could decide what to play with.

Suddenly Spot had an idea.
"I know," he said. "Let's
go camping!"

"But it's wet outside," said Helen.
"Yes," said Steve. "How can we go
camping in the rain?"
"I'll show you," said Spot, who was
already rushing out of the door with
a blanket. "Follow me – and bring
the torch."

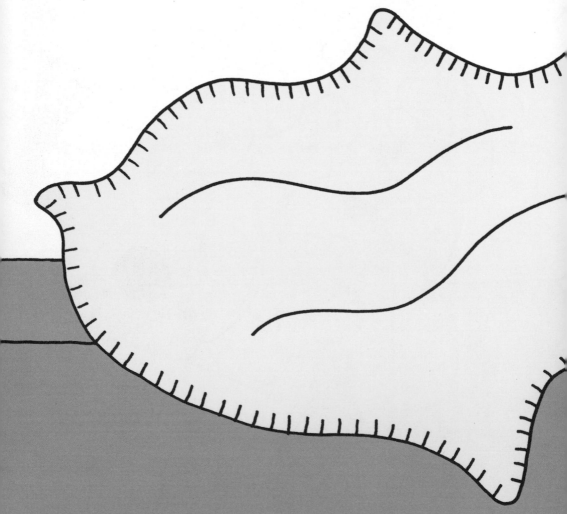

Spot pulled some chairs out into the middle of the kitchen. He put the blanket over them.

"This will be our tent," he said.
"We can pretend we're in
the woods."
"The table can be the trees!"
said Helen.

Spot and Steve crawled into the tent.
"It's just like a real tent," said Steve.
"And look! We can make shadows with
the torch."

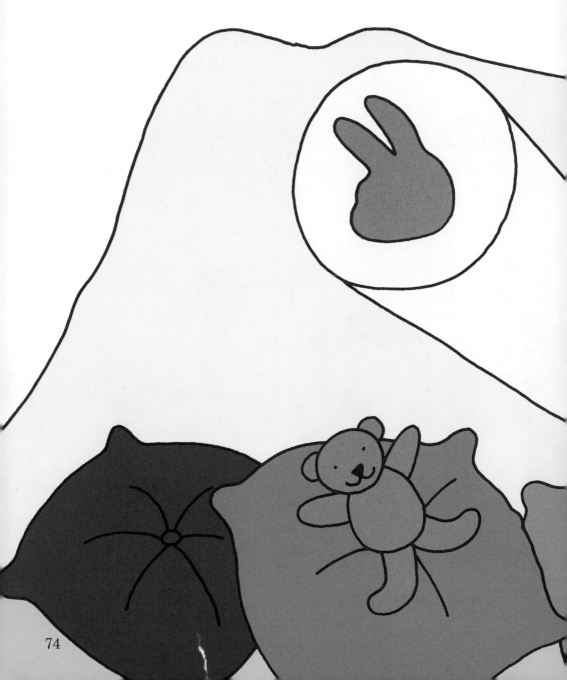

Steve and Spot had fun making lots of different shadows. Spot made a shadow that looked like a mouse. Steve made a shadow that looked like a rabbit.

All at once, Spot and Steve realised
that Helen wasn't there.
"Where can she be?" Spot wondered.

"I don't know," said Steve.
"But what's that noise?"
There was a strange growling
coming from outside the tent!

Steve and Spot peeped out to see what the noise was.
"It's me!" said Helen.
"I'm pretending to be a bear!"
Spot and Steve laughed.

"I thought it was my tummy growling," said Spot, "because I'm hungry. If we're camping, we should have a picnic."

"Did you say picnic?" said a voice.
It was Spot's mum – bringing a picnic
basket filled with yummy food.

"Thanks, Mum," said Spot. "You're just in time. I think my tummy really was starting to sound like a very big, angry bear!"

Spot, Steve and Helen shared all the sandwiches and fruit. And there was a surprise at the bottom of the picnic basket.

"Biscuits!" said Helen.
"My favourites," said Spot. "This is
a perfect picnic."

"This is so much fun," said Steve.
"I hope it never stops raining."
"But it has stopped," said Helen.
The sun was shining through the kitchen
window – and there was a beautiful
rainbow in the sky.

"Great!" said Spot, gathering up
the blanket. "Now we can go camping
for real."
"In the woods?" asked Steve.
"No," said Spot, "In the garden.
And this time I'm going to be
the bear!"

"Hooray!" they all cried, rushing outside for their next camping adventure.

Spot's
New Game

Spot and Tom were in the garden.
"When you've finished on the swing,
can we play a game?" asked Tom.
"OK," said Spot. "Let's play
hide-and-seek."
"That's not much fun with just the
two of us," said Tom.

Just then, Helen and Steve looked over the fence.

"Yoo-hoo, Spot!" said Helen.
"Can we play with you and Tom?"
"Yes!" said Spot. "We can play
hide-and-seek. You can hide and
I'll shut my eyes and count to ten.
Then watch out!"

Spot started to count. Helen, Tom
and Steve ran around finding
places to hide.
"One, two, three…" said Spot.

95

"Where shall I hide?" said Helen.
Tom and Steve had disappeared
and Spot was still counting.
"Four, five, six…" said Spot.
Then, Helen found a hiding place.

"Seven, eight, nine…ten!" Spot opened his eyes. "Here I come!" Spot looked around. There was no sign of Helen, or Tom, or Steve.

Spot looked behind the fence.
"Nobody there," said the blue bird,
as it flew away.
Spot walked past a rose bush.
"Mmm, that's a nice smell,"
said Spot.
Then Spot stopped. He heard a noise
coming from behind the bush. It was
a giggle – definitely a giggle!

"I've never heard a bush giggle,"
said Spot, and he looked behind
the bush.
"Found you, Helen!" said Spot.
"I heard you giggle."
"Oops!" said Helen. "I was enjoying
myself too much!"

Spot carried on looking for the others, but there was no sign of Tom or Steve. Spot even looked inside the wheelbarrow.
"You woke me up!" said Ginger cat. "I was having a nice dream."
"Sorry!" said Spot.

Spot went a bit further
down the garden path and
stopped by a tree. He heard
another giggle.
"I haven't heard a tree giggle, either,"
said Spot.
He looked up and shouted,
"Come down, Steve! I heard
you giggle."

Steve jumped down from
the tree.
"Have you found Tom yet?"
he asked.
"Not yet," said Spot.
Suddenly, a loud noise came
from the shed and a rabbit
jumped out from behind a
flowerpot. Then Spot heard
another giggle.

Spot opened the shed door and there was Tom.

"What was that noise?" asked Spot.
"Oh, I was giggling so much I knocked down a flowerpot," said Tom.
"I like this game... if only I could stop giggling!"

111

"Well," said Spot, "now that I've found everyone, I think we should play the game again. That was fun."
Helen smiled.
"Yes, but this time we can call the game hide-and-giggle!"
And that started off another round of giggles.

Happy Birthday, Spot

Spot woke up happy and excited.
Today was his birthday! He rushed down
to his breakfast.
"Happy birthday, Spot!" said Sally and
Sam. "You've got a lot of cards!"

Spot opened his cards and then
had breakfast. It was fun having
a birthday, and his friends were
coming for tea later on.
"Are you making a cake for my
birthday, Mum?" asked Spot.
"Yes," said Sally. "A very special one.
Would you like to help me?"

"Yes, please!" said Spot. "I'd like to do the icing – all different colours!"
"All right, let's start," said Sally.

Sally started to make the cake. Ginger cat wanted to help as well.

"I don't think we need your help, Ginger cat," said Sally. "But you can help me clean up afterwards."

Sam came into the kitchen.
"It's so nice outside," he said.
"We should have your party in
the garden, Spot."
"Good idea, Dad!" said Spot.
"I'll help you to get everything
ready."

Spot and Sam hung balloons and
streamers all over the garden.
It looked very colourful.
"This is my best birthday ever!"
 said Spot.

Spot finished in the garden and went to the kitchen. There was a lovely smell.
"You can do the icing now, Spot," said Sally.

"And when you've done that, you can put the candles on the cake. Then we're nearly ready."

As Spot put the last candle on the
cake, he heard the doorbell ring.
He ran to the door and there were
Tom, Helen and Steve holding
brightly wrapped presents.
"Happy birthday, Spot!"
they all said.

Spot couldn't wait to open his presents!
There was a new ball from Steve
and a big box of crayons from Tom.
Helen had brought Spot a jigsaw
with a picture of a farm.

"Thank you for my presents!"
said Spot, giving each of his
friends a big hug. "They're just
what I wanted!"

Then Spot and his friends went out to the garden to play their favourite games until it was time for tea.

133

Sally brought out all the food and everyone put on party hats. "Sausages!" said Tom. "They are my favourites!"

"And jelly and ice cream!" said Steve.
"And wait until you see the cake!"
said Spot. "I helped to make it."

At last Sally and Sam brought in the birthday cake – with a special surprise on top!

"Look!" Helen exclaimed. "It's a little Spot, made of icing sugar!"

"And I thought I was the one who did the icing," laughed Spot.
Sam lit the candles and everyone sang, "Happy Birthday."
Spot was very happy.

With one great big puff, Spot blew out
every single candle. Then he closed
his eyes to make his birthday wish.
Everyone cheered.
"What did you wish for, Spot?"
asked Helen.
"I can't tell you," said Spot.
"If I did, it wouldn't come true!"

Everyone cheered again.
"Happy birthday, Spot! We hope
you get your wish!"